MIRANDA ELAINE

AMIE KNIGHT

Millie

THERE IS A SUDDEN RUSH OF ADRENALINE YOU FEEL before going on stage in front of fans who have spent their time and money to come out to see you perform. I feel it every time I take the stage, and tonight, is no exception. Knowing that tens of people have shown up to hear me sing gets my blood pumping and my excitement to an all-time high. I just know that the show tonight will be the one to change my entire future. I've been singing here every Sunday night for the last five months, and I truly feel that my fan base is starting to grow. Why else would all of these people come to the only bar on this side of town every week? Surely, at least one of them has some sort of connection in the music industry and can help me kick-start my career.

Walking into Bill's BAR-B-Q House, I'm eager to get out there and do my thing. Ever since I was a little girl and got a toy microphone for Christmas, I knew I was destined to be on a stage—singing my heart out. It's my dream, and this bar is the first step in my detailed plan to become a famous pop singer. So what if the first step is my town's hole-in-the-wall watering hole slash barbecue joint? Hey, even Britney had to start somewhere, right?

Bill's is the kind of dive bar you'd find in every small town. Dark wooden panels adorn the walls, and pictures from the thirty years it's been open cover every inch of space available. Smoke fills the air, and beer fills cold, frosty glasses. Bill and his wife, Susie, have owned the bar since before I was born, but their son, Joel, has been running it for the last few years since they decided to finally retire.

If you are here before seven, it's probably for a big plate of barbecue with a side of collard greens. But, if it's after nine, then you are here for pitchers of beer, shootin' darts, and catching up with everyone. We might only be thirty miles from the big city, but if you grew up here, you'd know that it might as well be a whole other state. This town hasn't changed in decades, and I honestly don't expect it to adapt to modern life anytime soon. There isn't much room for growth in Sugar Hill.

Even with Joel's attempts to add new life to the place, the bar is mostly still the same kind of dive it's always been. Where a few pinball machines used to sit, Joel has set up a small stage. The stage is now my main reason for getting dolled up and getting my ass here at nine p.m. every Sunday night.

Nothing about the place is particularly special; it's like any other dive bar. The dusty, old jukebox I used to love when my daddy would bring me and my sister here every Saturday afternoon still sits in the corner. Back then, I loved coming here. We'd eat peanuts—and of course we could just throw the shells right down on the floor—and play music while twirling around the tiny dance floor. Some of my favorite childhood memories happened right here in this dark and dirty bar, and now, my adult dreams play out every Sunday night when I take the stage.

"Hey, sweet lady. You ready for tonight?" Joel shouts over to me as I walk in the door.

I've known him since we were kids, and I'm pretty sure he's had a crush on me for just as long. A fact I've got no problem using to my advantage to kick-start my career and get a prime spot in the Sunday night lineup.

"Hi, Joel. How's it going? Good crowd tonight?" I ask as I make my way to the bar. "What's the lineup like for tonight?"

"A couple newbies going on before you as of now. Whatcha singing for us tonight?" he replies with a wink and a sexy smirk.

I'd fall for his charm if I didn't have bigger goals. I am not about to start mixing business with pleasure, and Bill's is my main joint for gigs.

"I'm thinking it's a 'Toxic' kind of night. You got the track?"

"Yeah, babe. I got you. We got all the Britney songs. I wouldn't let you down like that."

A few of the old men shake their heads, but whatever. Britney is classic and they are just out of touch. Plus, I put my own spin on every song. I'll win them all over in the end. I have no doubt about it.

The typical weekend crowd is out tonight. Old men escaping their nagging wives, guys I went to school with looking for a quick lay, and tramped-up girls eager to give it to them. I know them all, and at the same time, I don't. With a dad who was in and out of jail for conning people and a momma who left before I could walk, my family was not the most well received. No one wants to be friends with the con artist's daughter. Anyway, I'm more focused on furthering my singing career than worrying about men and dating. I know that, after my pop album goes number one, I will have time to worry about silly things like boys, dating, and losing my virginity.

I look around and see only one unfamiliar face nursing a bottle of Budweiser in the corner. And trust me, this is a face I will not soon forget. He's strikingly handsome, in the works-for-a-living sort of way. His tight, black T-shirt shows off the kinds of muscles you only get from working hard. His deeply tanned skin is accentuated by dark hair and deep-brown eyes. He's the kind of man young girls dream about and grown women lust over. I may be innocent, but I'm no stranger to a fantasy. The moment I lay my eyes on him, I know he will soon star in every single one I have for the foreseeable future. I can't help but stare for a moment more before forcing myself to turn away and focus on why I am here.

"I bet even you would ride that man like a prize-winning stallion," someone says behind me.

Glancing over my shoulder, I see Hannah, my roommate and only real friend. She also happens to be the town whore, but who am I to judge? If she is happy, then I am happy. We couldn't be more different, yet we just work. She is my biggest cheerleader, always showing up to my gigs —though she never leaves them alone—and I make sure to pick her up a large box of condoms on the weeks I go to the grocery store.

"You ain't wrong," I agree, stunning Hannah—because I never show interest in the men around here.

You try being labeled a criminal just because of who your family is and then you'll see how many men are waiting to beat your door down. I find it's best to keep my nose down and focus on my goals—like getting out of this podunk town.

I make my way past the stage and the bar, toward the small prep area in the back. I share the space with the other female performers and patrons who are touching their lipstick up or relieving themselves of the several bottles of beer they have already consumed this evening. It's not an ideal situation, but I'm going to make the most of the night. I grab my makeup bag and my hairbrush and make sure I'm picture ready. You never know who might snap a quick shot to post to social media, and I am not one to turn free press down. I tease my blond hair out, which has somehow fallen flat between when I left my house and arrived at the bar. Then I reapply my signature hot-pink lipstick.

With my makeup fixed and a new coat of hair spray ensuring that every hair stays in place, I am ready to make my entrance. I head out of the dressing room, toward the main stage. Before I can register what is happening, my hands are yanked behind my back and a pair of handcuffs are slapped on my wrists. I find my body pressed up against the hall wall, and what feels like a large, well-built man has pushed up behind me, rubbing his hands all over my body.

"You're coming with me," he growls out.

Then it finally registers what's happening.

"Shit. Not again," I groan.

Chapter 2

JAKE

"Stay still, Tillie. I'm sick and tired of chasing your crazy ass around town," I snarl out to the insane female I have pressed up against the wall.

A perfectly round ass is wiggling all too enticingly against my already hardening cock, and I let out an exasperated sigh. Stupid dick. Clearly, it doesn't know what's good for us. Peppermint and some kind of floral soap assail my senses. I almost back away so I can take a harder look at this blonde bombshell, but I refuse to be fooled again. I've been hunting this woman down for weeks, and every time I've managed to catch up with her, she has somehow managed to give me the slip. Not again. She missed her court date, and it's my job to bring her in. I have something to prove, being the new guy on the block. I've only been on the job for two weeks, and I've spent most of it chasing this criminally deranged woman. True, her crimes consist mostly of bounced checks and small thefts, but the way she has managed to evade me these past two weeks only proves one thing—she's a damn criminal mastermind.

"I'm not Tillie, you big oaf. Let me go. Now!" the crazy lady says while trying to turn her body toward me.

I press her harder into the wall with my body and groan. Fuck, she feels too good. She's trying to kill me. I've been stabbed, beaten, and shot at plenty in my six years as a bounty hunter, but I've never been more convinced that someone was trying to kill me than at this moment. And she is using that smoking-hot body as the weapon. Fuck my life.

Funnily enough, I've never once felt this pull toward Tillie while I've been tracking her. But, now that I am up close and personal, I cannot help but want her. Everything about her is calling to me. Her voice, her smell—this woman is fucking intoxicating.

"Cut the bullshit, darlin'. I've been watching you for weeks now and you know it. I watched you walk in this door not ten minutes ago. I'm taking you in, collecting my money, and getting a good night's sleep tonight." I'm so over this shit.

"God dammit, let me go. I am *not* Tillie." She's talking to the wall, but I'm mostly paying attention. "I'm Millie, and you are ruining my gig. My fans are expecting me up on stage any minute," she says.

I take a look around this dive of a bar that smells like bacon and stale beer, trying to hold my smirk back. Grabbing the handcuffs around Tillie's wrists, I spin her around to face me.

"Babe, karaoke is *not* a gig, and if you think it is, then we got bigger problems than a few bounced checks and some petty theft charges," I say, taking in her curvy body, starting at the tips of her pink-painted toes. I want to pull those gorgeous toes out of the high-heeled sandals she's wearing and take a nibble, but I know that, the moment she thinks I'm distracted, she'll take off on me again.

My eyes make their way up smooth, tanned legs until I hit the hem of her pale-blue dress with white polka dots right above her knees. And damn, that dress perfectly hugs every curve of her body. My hand almost involuntary makes its way up to the long strand of pearls dangling around her neck. I want to pull her closer with them so I can smell her again or maybe run my tongue over her plump, pink-stained lips. Big, angry, bright-blue eyes snap me out of my lust-fueled fog. Fuck. This girl is fucking gorgeous, and I immediately know I won't be taking her in right away.

"You're new around here, aren't you?" she snaps at me, the ice in her blue gaze freezing me.

The corners of my mouth tip up in a barely there smile. God, I love a sassy woman.

She leans her upper body closer to me until our noses are almost touching. "Get your sexy ass on the phone with Manny now. Go on. Call your boss. He'll tell you. You have the wrong girl," she says, her breath ghosting across my lips.

I couldn't disagree with her more. I have the right girl, and I cannot wait to get her home and into my bed.

"You think I'm sexy?" I smirk down at her.

Her eyes narrow, making a small wrinkle appear between her eyebrows, and I can't help but chuckle. She's fucking adorable.

"Get Manny on the fucking phone right now, whatever the hell your name is. You're keeping my fans waiting," she snarls out two inches from my face.

"Babe, my name is Jake Blackwood, and the last thing I wanna do right now is call Manny."

Her eyes flutter closed, and I feel her breath hitch against my chest. I softly brush my lips against her bottom lip. A low growl rumbles in my chest, and I know that this is what heaven feels like.

The ringing of my cell phone surprises me and I jerk away from Tillie.

"Stay." I point to her, letting her know I mean business.

I get a heavy eye roll and a frustrated sigh as I look down at my phone. Manny.

I answer the phone with a simple, "Yeah."

"Did you get her yet?" he asks.

I know exactly who he is talking about, and I've finally gotten her, but now that I have her, the last thing I want to do is take her in. I look over at Tillie and smile at the way the handcuffs pull her arms back and push her breasts forward.

"Yeah. I picked her up at Bill's. She's giving me a little trouble, but I'll have her in shortly," I say into the phone, making sure to keep my eyes on Tillie. I'm lying. I am definitely not taking her in. I'm taking her home.

Manny lets out a frustrated groan. "Jake, Tillie doesn't hang out at Bill's. However, Millie, her twin sister, does. I'm willing to bet you got the wrong girl, bro." He lets out a heavy sigh. "It's not a thing, man. It's happened to all of us. They look just alike, only Millie has a heart-shaped birthmark on her inner upper thigh. Check it out before you bother bringing her in."

The line goes dead, and I know that I am fucked. Tillie

or Millie or whoever the fuck this sexy-as-hell broad is gives me a told-you-so smile, and I want to kiss it right off her face. I put my cell in my back pocket and drop to my knees in front of her.

She looks down at me, smiling, lifting her right leg, and placing her right heel on my shoulder. I take both hands and run them up her calf, past her knee, pushing her dress up along the way. And, sure enough, on the inside of her right thigh is a heart. I run my finger over it and savor the moment. I can smell her wet heat, and my mouth is too close to it. I want to run my nose over the crotch of her silky, blue underwear peeking from beneath her dress. I want to lap up her sweetness and relish every inch of her silky, smooth skin with my mouth.

Except there is plenty of time for that later. When we are alone. In my bedroom. So, I wrap my arm around the bottom of her gorgeous ass and haul her up and over my shoulder. I stand up and start marching toward the parking lot, trying to ignore the screeching Millie thrown over my shoulder.

"Put me down this minute, Jake Blackwood. You know damn well I'm not Tillie. This is kidnapping! I am going to tell Manny as soon as you put me down, you bastard!" she screams at the top of her lungs.

Everyone in Bill's is giving us wild stares, but I couldn't care less. I give Millie's ass a hard smack and turn my head to it. It's situated so close to my face. I can't help but give it a firm bite, which only causes her to wiggle and fight more. I smile. This is fun.

"Calm yourself, woman. We are going home, where you

can do all the yelling you want from between my sheets," I say, giving her ass one more smack for good measure.

Tonight's turned out to be a good night after all. I'll take Millie home and make her think that, if she can get Tillie to turn herself in, I'll let her go. Only that's not happening. Because I'm keeping Millie. She's mine.

Chapter 3

Millie

"Hey! Muscles! Over here!" Hannah yells behind us in the parking lot of Bill's.

I see her running upside down behind us through the parking lot. Okay, maybe *I'm* the one upside down, dangling from the defined shoulder of my abductor.

"Muscles! I said Muscles, stop!" Hannah shouts out once more.

We come to an abrupt halt.

"You talkin' to me, sweets?" Jake growls out.

I can't help but feel a tinge of jealousy over his term of endearment for my friend.

"You see anyone else built like a freaking brick wall, handsome? I don't think so," Hannah says when she catches up to us, eyeing my Jake up and down.

My Jake? WTF? Can Stockholm Syndrome hit that fast? I guess, with being twenty-four and a virgin, my hormones were bound to kick in at some point.

"Han, get me off this big lug. I'm being kidnapped! Tell Jake Blackwood I can't get him Tillie." I squirm and kick, desperately trying to free myself, while my so-called best friend eye-fucks the man who has taken me hostage.

This is not the first time I have been mistaken for my sister by someone she has wronged, and every time, they think I am the key to nabbing her. I need to get free. He is keeping me from the biggest turnout at a gig I've ever had. There were at least fifteen people inside the bar, waiting for my performance.

Hannah completely ignores my pleas, and thanks to what is clearly an extreme devotion to the gym, Jake's grip on my ass has not loosened the tiniest bit. I am no closer to freedom than I was before she arrived, but at least I have the delicious view of his firm ass from up here. An ass, I might add, that has me all kinds of worked up, especially when paired with the rest of his overly hot body and smoldering good looks. It might be a good thing he has a good hold on me because I am a bit weak in the knees.

I twist the top half of my body around Jake and make eye contact with my devilish former best friend. I know she is up to something, and her intentions cannot be good, considering where her moral compass lies. She smirks my way before planting her palm on his chest and rubbing up and over his free shoulder.

"WOW! You really do earn your nickname," she says to Jake.

"Sweets, you need something or can me and my girl here be on our way?" he asks in a huff.

"All right, Muscles," she purrs out, and the hand she was resting on his shoulder glides all the way down his back and grips his ass hard before sliding into his pocket. She then pulls her hand out and gives his ass one more firm squeeze.

"Remember: No glove, no love. Be safe." She winks at me and skips—yes, like a small child—all the way back into the bar.

I cannot even begin to fathom what she is thinking. He could be a murderer and she is giving him a condom *I* bought *her*. UGH. She is totally out of my thank-you Grammys speech. *OUT.*

"Not cool, Han! Not cool!" I yell out after her as she disappears into the bar.

Chuckling, Jake walks us to an overly large, black SUV. This could totally be worse. He could be taking me to a dirty, white van with tinted windows. My friend, Flint, drives one of *those* vans, and while he is a nice enough guy, it absolutely terrifies me. At least it's not a rape van, I tell myself.

"Trying to make up for shortcomings, Jake Blackwood?" I can't help but mock him.

Suddenly, he lowers me to the ground and pushes my back up against the car. With my hands still cuffed behind my back and Jake holding a firm grip on my hips, I'm unable to flee or fight. Before I can comprehend what's happening, he pushes his hard body against mine and a very hard cock is pressing firmly into my belly. Instantly, my panties are soaked and I'm breathing so hard that you would think I had just run a marathon.

"Okay, darlin'," he whispers into my neck, his hard body up against me in the best way possible. "This is how it's all goin' down. You're coming home with me and helping me find that sneaky-ass sister of yours, and then, when all that is settled, I'm gonna prove to you that there isn't one shortcoming anywhere on my body. You feel me?" He yanks the door beside me open and gently shoves me inside before I can reply.

Jake leans over me, grabs the seat belt, and surprises me by carefully buckling me into place. I am too stunned to move or fight. I should struggle and run, but something about this man keeps me planted firmly in the seat. He starts this mammoth of a car and heads to God knows where.

"We're here," Jake barks at me.

We pull up to a house only fifteen minutes out of town, but it's too far away from my dreams of stardom. After he rounds the car and opens my door, he leads me to a simple craftsman-style house. Clearly, a bachelor lives here. There is not a decoration or inspiration board in sight. There is no way a woman has *ever* lived here—a thought that alarmingly makes me giddy inside. I yank my cuffed hands away from his hold so I can spin to look him in the eye.

"Look, Mr. I-Can-Just-Up-and-Kidnap-a-Girl-Because-I-Have-a-Shiny-Bounty Hunter-Badge. You need to take me back to Bill's right away. I could be wasting my big shot," I spurt at him, squinting in annoyance.

"Darlin', until you get Tillie here and in my custody, you ain't goin' nowhere. So cuddle up on the couch and make yourself comfortable, 'cause you are here for the long haul," Jake informs me, a smile on his face. He takes my elbow in his hand to guide me toward the living room and gives me a small shove so I fall backward onto his couch.

"Jake Blackwood, this is not funny! I haven't seen my sister since she stole my crutches and sold them to the pawn shop when I sprained my ankle three months ago," I tell him with a small stomp of my foot. I feel my anger rise as I continue to explain the seriousness of the situation. "Do you know how hard it is to practice choreographed dance routines hopping on one foot? Well, let me tell you, it is no easy feat, but I just kept telling myself if Britney can get through two thousand seven, then I can get through this. I just hobbled along to the YouTube tutorial—"

"I get it," he rudely interrupts as I attempt to explain the hardships I have to endure while having a twin like Tillie. The struggle is real, and he needs to know that, while I may be older than she is by two minutes, we are not close. She has never listened to a thing I've told her.

"Still, y'all are sisters and there has to be a way for you to get that cunning woman here. Figure it out, darlin'," he says easily—like he just didn't demand a damn miracle from me.

This arrogant ass thinks I'm just gonna do what he says because he snaps his fingers? Who does he think he is? Justin Timberlake? Nope. Although, to be fair, Jake would never need to bring sexy back since I don't think it left him in the first place. A man like Jake has never had to endure an awkward stage. Every inch of him is manly, rugged, and defined. He has the kind of pure, robust sexuality that just comes naturally to a select few.

Even though I'm being held here against my will, all I can think about is what his skin tastes like and how firm his abs are behind that tight, black T-shirt. Shit, I'm sweating. I have never been one to let men distract me from practicing, perfecting, and performing my craft, but something about him makes me not care about the missed opportunity at the bar tonight. Despite the hell I am giving him for it.

"Well, there is no way I can get ahold of her tonight. Am I supposed to just sit here all night, handcuffed while watching you brood and pout about constantly being outsmarted, or are you gonna show me to my room?" I ask through gritted teeth.

"Like hell you're stayin' in any bed but mine!" he exclaims. "I don't need you sneaking out in the middle of the night and taking the first lead I've had on your slippery sister with you. You're sleeping in my bed. Next to me."

I should fight him on this. I just met him. All I know about him is his name and the fact that he works for Manny and has it out for my sister. But the idea of him shirtless in bed all night excites me in ways I've never felt before. I want to know what it would be like to wake up curled in his arms, his powerful thighs intertwined with mine. I want to feel nothing but his cotton pants and my sliver of barely there panties separating us. I want it so much that I am starting to drool. I'll play his game, but I have no desire to make this easy for him.

"Fine. But I have no intention of falling asleep smelling like a bar. I need a shower and something to sleep in. You got any spare shirts lying around? Or have you Hulk-ripped them all apart in fits of rage whenever criminal masterminds slip away into the night?" I grumble at Jake.

He mumbles under his breath in what I can only describe as a series of vowels mixed with curse words and closes the space separating us. He releases the handcuffs that have held me captive since the bar. His strong brow puckers with concern. Noticing the red lines on my wrists, he gently grabs them and runs his thumbs over the marks.

"Shower is the first door on the left. I'll grab you a shirt," he says much more gently than he has spoken all night.

My eyes meet his, and I hold his stare for a moment more before turning and making my way to the bathroom.

Just as I finish undressing, he yanks the door open, hardly giving me enough time to jump in the shower and hide behind the curtain.

"Towel and shirt are on the counter, and the door stays open. I don't need you trying to shimmy that cute ass of yours out the window," he says softly.

He finally leaves, and I pop my head out and around the curtain. He left the door freaking wide open. Knowing there is nothing to be done about it at this point, I let it go. With the hot water pouring down over my head, I let the craziness of this day go and relax the best way I know how. I grab the shampoo bottle and let free my best Britney song.

Chapter 4

JAKE

I'M NOT GETTING A GODDAMN WINK OF SLEEP TONIGHT. Millie's luscious body is going to keep me awake all night long. A man doesn't lie in bed that close to a woman who looks like Millie and sleep. I'll gladly suffer through it, though, to make her mine. I make quick work of taking my T-shirt and jeans off and putting my sleep pants on. I usually sleep in the nude, but I'll need to ease Millie into that. Or maybe not. While Millie may not be a criminal mastermind, she damn sure *is* a raving lunatic. The shrieking coming from the bathroom only proves it. She's a refreshing surprise, and the truth is I never know what's going to come out of her crazy-ass mouth. I like it.

Maybe I even love it a little, which absolutely terrifies me. I've never felt such an instant connection to a woman before in my life. Sure, I've been with plenty of females, but never in a serious relationship. I've definitely never felt this instantaneous attraction that I do with Millie.

The shrieking stops when the shower does, but I can still hear her humming as she towels off. When I've given her enough time to get dressed, I make my way to the bathroom and stand in the doorway, looking my fill. Of course she looks like a wet dream standing in front of the mirror in nothing besides one of the standard black shirts I wear almost every day. Her skin is still pink from the shower. She's brushing her wet, tangled locks with my hairbrush, and I feel my chest fill with all the things that I want her to have of mine. I want her to cook meals in my kitchen, lounge on my couch next to me and watch my TV, and, most importantly, sleep in my bed. Beside me. For some crazy reason, I feel fiercely protective and loyal to this ridiculous woman. I've lost my damn mind.

A drop of water slowly makes its way from her hairline down her neck, and before I can even think about it, the front of my body is pressed closely to the back of hers. My hard cock rests firmly between her ass cheeks. Fuck, I'm ninety-nine percent sure she isn't wearing any underwear. If I thought my cock was hard before, I was *so* wrong. I lean my head around hers and slide my tongue from the sweet spot between her neck and her shoulder all the way to her ear, lapping up her sweetness. I nip her lobe. I watch us in the mirror, her head tipped to the side, allowing me to take my fill. Her face is wild and uninhibited. My big body hovers over and all around her, and I feel that crazy bout of protectiveness surge through my body again.

"You done with your Christina Aguilera impressions, babe? Or do I need to get some earmuffs before we go to bed?" I whisper into her ear, smiling.

All of a sudden, Millie spins in my arms, her eyes throwing daggers my way. She uses her tiny, curvy body to push me back into the doorjamb. She thinks she can muscle *me* into a corner? I feel a smile hit my lips as I let her.

"No, Jake Blackwood. Never Christina. Never! It's Britney, bitch," she says two inches from my face.

This girl. She is a damn nut. And I can't contain the bubbles of laughter that rumble out of me. Placing my hands on Millie's shoulders, I move her back a little and bend over in laughter, holding my stomach. Seriously, this chick is certifiable, but I haven't laughed this hard in years. It feels good.

"I don't care *who* it is, darlin', but I think the general consensus is America *don't* got talent," I say, standing up and wiping tears of laughter from my eyes.

I straighten to my full height bringing my eyes to Millie's, expecting to see anger. Only, once again, she surprises me. Her eyes are full of teasing, and her mouth holds the hint of a small smile. I get the strangest feeling that maybe Millie knows she is a little crazy and has absolutely no fucks to give about it. And that thought only makes me like her more.

She backs up, slides her body down the vanity, and sits on the floor, letting out a big sigh. I mimic her, sliding down the doorjamb and sitting opposite her. Her tanned, naked legs tangle with my pajama-clad ones. My T-shirt rides up on her, revealing soft, supple thighs, and I spot the heart birthmark again. I want to lick it. I want to suck it. I want to…

"I know I'm not that good at singing, Jake Blackwood," she says, breaking me out of my thoughts.

I stare at her pretty blue eyes and give her an encouraging nod to keep going.

"I just want to be something someday, ya know? Something more than a con man's daughter. Something more than the town criminal's sister. I just want to be something more," she finishes on a whisper.

My chest aches a little at her words, and I rub the palm of my hand over my heart, trying to ease the burn there. I want to tell her that she's the type of person who can be anything she wants to be. That, if she wants more, she should just go out and get it. That she's just crazy enough to make shit happen. Except I don't want her out there with the rest of the world. I want her in here. With me. But I don't let my selfishness get the best of me.

"You can be anything you want to be, Millie Coletrain, and don't ever let anyone tell you different," I say, my deep voice echoing off the bathroom walls even though I said it quietly.

"Yeah?" she asks, her voice hopeful.

I nod, watching her face light up. My scalp prickles and tingles at that smile, and I run my hand through my hair, feeling like the crazy fucker I am acting like.

"And what is it that *you* want?" she asks me seriously.

I eye her from the tip of her toes all the way up to the blond hair on her head. My gaze slowly sweeps over her, taking in every facet of her. I want to memorize her sitting on my bathroom floor, her heart in her eyes, spilling her feelings to me. I know that my answer is in my eyes.

"How old are you, Jake?" she asks, picking imaginary lint off my T-shirt.

Jake. Just Jake. Not Jake Blackwood. Warmth settles into my chest.

"Thirty-one. You?" I ask even though I already know. I know Tillie's workup like the back of my hand, and they are twins, after all.

"Twenty-four, and I have no fucking clue what I am doing with my life," she says through sad laughter.

I push my legs closer to hers, trying to offer her the little comfort I can. She smiles shyly at me.

"What's your favorite color?" I ask because I want to know everything about this woman. From her favorite foods to her biggest dreams. I want it all.

"Pink, naturally," she says with a bit of sass, and I chuckle.

"Naturally." I nod through my laughter. Because she's right. It makes perfect sense.

"What's yours?" she asks, sitting forward like she really wants to know.

It's been a long time since a chick wanted to know something about me other than the size of my biceps and my dick.

"Used to be black." I grin. "Now, it's blue," I say, staring intensely into her eyes.

She diverts her eyes, and I see the blush hit her chest, move up her neck, and land on her face. That blush and her smile do me in. I'm rock hard and my insides are lit up like a fucking Christmas tree. Fuck, I want her. Now.

"Time for bed, darlin'," I say before getting up off the floor and scooping her up under her ass and her back.

"Jake Blackwood, you can't just go around manhandling women. I can walk to the bed just fine on my own two feet!" she yells, wrapping her arms around my neck.

This one. All bark. No bite. I smile and shake my head as she wraps herself around me and settles her body against mine like I'm her personal teddy bear.

I pull the navy sheets on my bed back and lay her

beneath them. I cover her up to her chin and run my index finger along the bridge of her nose. She closes her eyes and snuggles down with a sigh. Fucking adorable.

I climb in on the other side of the bed and scoot over to Millie, plastering my body right up against hers. I wrap my arm around her waist, pulling her back and closer to me until we're spooning, her back to my front. She grunts a little and stiffens, but eventually, she melts back into me. We fit together like two puzzle pieces. I take a moment to breathe her in and enjoy the contrast of her soft to my hard.

After sliding my right hand under my pillowcase and my left hand down the length of her arm, I grab her hand and gently pull it up toward the top of my bed, where I snap a pair of handcuffs around her wrist and the steel bar of the headboard. The clank of metal against metal as Millie jiggles her hand is ominous, and I know that a shitstorm is headed my way.

"You did not just handcuff me to this bed, Jake Blackwood!" she exclaims into the quiet of my bedroom. She jiggles her hand again, creating more of the awful metal banging sound.

"Stop pulling your wrist before you hurt yourself. Now, darlin', I can't have you running off into the night. And besides, if I recall correctly, I still need to show you all of my non-shortcomings," I whisper before nipping her ear.

Millie

"YOU CAN'T JUST CUFF ME TO YOUR BED!" I YELL AT HIM again. My frustration at being handcuffed *again* by this man has me fighting against the handcuffs, causing them to jingle yet again.

I hear him chuckle behind me. I cannot believe the audacity of this man.

Before I can continue my argument, he presses into my ass once more, his massive erection rubbing against me in the most blissful way. My body wants to push back, desperate for more contact, but my head says to stay strong. He nips at my ear, and I can feel the smile on his lips. Jake moves to suck at my neck, causing me to instinctively tilt my head to the side to give him better access. I have a feeling my body is winning the war against my head. How have I gone this long in my life and not known about this amazingly sensitive spot? What else have I been missing out on?

"You're not foolin' me, darlin'. You like being handcuffed to my bed. I bet, if I slip my finger between those sweet thighs of yours, I'd find you drippin' wet. We might have some unfinished business dealing with your sister, but this. *Us.* It's happening." He smirks back at me.

I smile and blush like the virgin I am. I'm grateful Jake can't see the pink of my cheeks from behind me. I want tonight with him. Even if this is all I ever have of him, I want to give him what I have never given to another man. He's right. If he hadn't handcuffed me to the bed, I'd object. These cuffs give me the freedom to let go. I want this. I know I just met him, and the whole situation with him using me to get to Tillie is fucked up. Still, I can't help but give in—even if it's just for tonight.

Needing to let him know I'm ready for whatever he has planned, I scoot back into him, causing my ass to grind against his hard cock. He emits a loud groan from the contact. Suddenly, I find myself flat on my back, my arms still stretched above my head, with Jake looking down at me. He stares into my eyes, his gaze hooded and rich with lust.

"So beautiful," Jake whispers to himself. He grips the edge of his shirt I'm wearing and toys with it.

Jake gently rubs the hem of the shirt back and forth over my thighs, managing to keep it pulled down just enough to cover my bare sex. The feel of his rough hands rubbing over my soft thighs sends lightning bolts of pleasure straight to my sex. I never imagined that such a simple touch could elicit this kind of response from my body.

I'm so worked up that I'm barely able to breathe. No man has ever touched me like this. I've never wanted to be touched like this, but I think I might die if he stops. Gently gripping the edge of the shirt, he slowly pushes it all the way up and above my breasts. I let out a loud sigh of anticipation. His hooded eyes darken as he looks down at my almost completely naked body. With my hand cuffed to the bed, I have no way to move my body in an attempt to be modest. He has me in such a frenzy that I don't even want to try.

"So sweet," he rasps out in the most delicious and gravelly voice I've ever heard.

I grow wetter by the second, and his intense gaze locked on me lets me know he sees it. With his eyes focused solely on me, I can feel a blush spreading over my cheeks. I start to make a joke to break the tension, but before I can muster one up, he lightly grabs my breast and rubs his thumb over my pert nipple. I completely lose my ability to speak, and I close my eyes and give in to the new sensations.

"Fuckin' mine," he declares, lowering his head and fully cupping my breast in his hand. He sucks my firm nipple into his mouth.

With no warning, he bites down on it, causing my eyes to jerk open. When he stops momentarily, I realize I am desperate for him to continue.

"More, Jake! Please more!" I plead.

He resumes torturing me in the most exquisite way possible. Rotating between gentle sucks and sharp nips, he has me begging for this not to end. Spurred on by my eager body and my frenzied pleas, Jake starts working his way down my body, kissing the sensitive spots along the path but completely avoiding the direction I was expecting. Instead, he continues down until he reaches my foot. My skin tingles everywhere his lips touch. A shiver runs straight to my core with the simplest of touches. I jerk with surprise as he gingerly sucks at my toe then quickly releases it with a *pop*!

"Needed to do that since I first saw these pretty, pink

toes in those fuck-me heels," he says before placing one more tender kiss to the tip of my toe.

I never thought I could possibly be into anything involving feet, but watching him suck my toe was surprisingly erotic and has me anticipating what more he has in store.

My breathing begins to accelerate while I watch him. He crawls back up my body and rubs his hands along my legs all the way until he reaches the backs of my knees. He lifts my legs and places them over his shoulder. His tongue snakes out and swipes across his top lip, his gaze never leaving my pussy. I close my eyes, unable to watch him stare so intimately at my most private area.

"So fuckin' wet," he growls out as he runs a finger between the apex of my thighs. "You've been imagining my mouth here all night, haven't you? Thinking about what it will feel like when my tongue laps at your pussy. I promise the reality will be much better than your fantasies."

Before I'm able to protest, his finger is replaced by his mouth and his tongue gives a long, slow lick up my slit. My back arches off the bed the short distance the handcuffs will allow.

"Jake!" I yell out a moan, which only seems to encourage him.

Suddenly, he begins to go at me like a man starved, and all I can do is hold on tight to the sheets while he completely devours me. The sucking and licking sounds, the groans rumbling from his chest, and the way his face is so completely buried in my pussy only heighten my arousal. It feels so illicit. So incredibly raw and dirty. I feel a rapid build of tension with each lick. When I think I can take no more,

Jake sucks my clit into his mouth and pushes two fingers inside me. I explode with the most intense orgasm I have ever felt. Clearly, what I have been doing on my own was all wrong. Nothing has ever felt as good as Jake's mouth on my clit and his fingers inside me.

After the haze from my orgasm lifts, I see Jake stand from the bed and grab something from the side table drawer. Leaning over me, he quickly and gently removes the handcuffs and inspects my wrists. Once again, like earlier on the couch, he caresses the red marks left by the cuffs, but this time, he follows that by placing a loving kiss on each wrist.

"I'm not on the pill," I blurt out and sit upright, breaking the silence and ending the tender moment. I've never been in a post-orgasmic situation with another person and have no clue what protocol is here.

A burst of laughter emits from Jake as he looks down at me from his place next to the bed. "Babe, I'm not sure how much experience you've had. Honestly, I don't want to know because the thought of another man even getting a glance at what is mine has me beyond angry at myself for not finding you sooner. But me eating you like I've never tasted anything sweeter—that can't make a baby, darlin'!" he exclaims, a smile on his lips.

"I know that, Jake Blackwood!" I yell, my smile matching his own. "I may be a virgin, but I'm not completely dense. I just figured, before we go any further tonight, I should let you know."

"My girl is a nut," he says to himself. He walks to the other side of the bed and climbs in next to me. He yanks the bedspread up to cover us both.

I turn to face him, and he pulls me into him. I lay my head on his massive chest, and he wraps his arms around my body. I love how it feels to have his big body engulf my small one.

"Tonight was all about you. I have been imagining watching you come cuffed to my bed since I first put them on your wrists at Bill's. And trust me, darlin', the reality was better than I could've ever dreamed. But, now, I need rest. I spent all day chasin' that insane sister of yours and all night rock hard, watching you. I need sleep. Tomorrow, you'll get me Tillie, and then we will pick up where we left off tonight because I'm nowhere near done tastin' your sweet flavor," Jake explains. With a yawn, he tugs me even closer into him and closes his eyes before falling asleep quickly.

He says that this isn't ending anytime soon, but I worry that, once he has Tillie in custody, all of this sudden happiness I have found will be over. It seems silly to feel so attached to someone I just met, but I do. I hate the idea of waking up one day and Jake not being next to me.

As I look at him sleeping next to me, it's blatantly obvious that Jake could get any girl he wants. Why would he choose a small-town reject like me? After just one night with this man, I know I will never be the same. I was ready to hand my virginity over to him after just a few hours alone with him. I must be crazy, but I've never felt more at home and at peace than I do here, in Jake's house, and in his arms. I'm not ready to give this up. I will just need to prolong the chase a bit longer. I can become more to him than a tool to catch an elusive criminal. Thankfully, I have no clue where the good-for-nothing girl I call a sister is. He won't be able to get rid of me if he can't find her.

JAKE

"A**SS**. S**EAT**." I **NOD** M**ILLIE OVER TO THE BARSTOOL ON** the other side of the counter.

I might come off gruff or bossy, but I'm trying my damnedest to keep myself in check. Don't get me wrong. I'm in a fantastic mood. I slept like a damn baby last night. I guess the exhaustion from chasing Tillie around finally caught up with me. That and being pressed so closely to Millie all night.

I got up early this morning and went for a run, leaving a mostly naked Millie in my bed. It was hard, leaving her, but I want to take things slow with her. I could fuck her right now if I wanted to. But I want to do this right. I want her for the long haul. So, even though I want to bend her over this counter and take her long and hard from behind, I distract myself by making us breakfast.

"Bossy," she mutters under her breath while rubbing the sleep from her eyes and sitting on the stool on the other side of the counter.

I'm tall enough that I can see my T-shirt ride up her thighs and almost expose her gorgeous, bare pussy. I let out an involuntary groan and get back to pouring the eggs in the frying pan. Fuck me, but that run did nothing to take the edge off like I'd hoped.

I pour Millie a cup of coffee and set it in front of her. "You weren't complaining about my bossiness last night when my mouth was between your legs." I smirk and get back to stirring the eggs.

"I distinctly remember complaining when you handcuffed me to that bed, Jake Blackwood." Millie rolls her eyes.

My girl is full of sass this morning. I smile as I turn the eggs off and move them to a different burner. I make my way around the counter to her and spin her on the stool until she's facing me. I grab under her arms and lift her.

"Eek! Cold," she squeaks when her bare ass makes contact with the cold granite of the counter.

After running my tongue slowly across her bottom lip, I whisper, "I don't recall any complaining last night when my face was buried in your wet pussy." I run my tongue over her top lip and feel her body shiver against mine. "In fact, all I remember is how tight you were. How hot and wet you were for me. How you begged me not to stop." I run my hands up her thighs. "I bet you're already wet for me right now, too."

She opens her mouth on a gasp at my words, and I take advantage, slamming my mouth down onto hers. My tongue tastes every inch of her gorgeous mouth, and still, it isn't enough. God, but I could spend all day kissing the sass out of this woman. She lets out a pained groan when I pull back and lay my forehead to hers.

"Now, my girl remembers," I whisper across her lips. It

takes every bit of my restraint, but I pull her trembling body off the counter, set her back on her stool, and head back to the kitchen to finish making our plates.

Millie looks a little dazed when I pass her breakfast plate to her. She rubs her thighs together.

I let out a chuckle before saying, "So, here's the plan, darlin'. We're gonna call that sister of yours this morning and get her ass over here so I can take her in and be done with this whole thing."

Millie's face falls, and that tiny wrinkle between her eyebrows pops up. I sit on the stool next to her and turn her until she is facing me. I rub my thumb over that wrinkle.

"What's troubling you, sugar?" I ask.

She frowns and says, "I can't call Tillie. I don't have my phone. It's in my car at the club *you* kidnapped me from last night."

"Not a problem," I say, turning and digging into my breakfast. "I'll take you to get your phone, and then we'll call Tillie and get her to meet us somewhere." I look at Millie and then at her still full plate. "Eat up, babe. We have a big day ahead."

She looks thoughtful and a bit sad. I wish I knew what was going on in her head. She's an anomaly to me. My job requires me to be good at reading people, and usually, I am. But this girl? She's full of surprises. I think that's one of the reasons I like her so much.

"Jake, I can't spend all day chasing Tillie all over town with you. You don't seem to understand that Tillie will have zero fucks about you holding me hostage. Zero. The last I heard, she was mooching off some old man at a retirement home. She's not coming to my rescue anytime soon. Besides, I have work today, and I never miss work."

I love that she's enjoying my food. My girl likes to eat, and I like her curves. It's a win-win.

"You aren't going to work today, Millie. You're staying with me," I demand, but even though her mouth is full of eggs and toast, I can tell she is going to fight me.

She swallows and angles her body toward mine. "I am not missing work today. Do you hear me? I need this job. It's the only thing I do in this town that earns me any respect, and you will not take it from me. Do you understand?" she asks.

I immediately feel like an asshole. I remember our talk last night on the bathroom floor and think that maybe this is her way of being something more. I'd never hold her back from that.

"Okay, baby. Finish eating and I'll take you to get your purse and then to your house so you can change. Then we'll head to work." I place my plate in the sink and start heading for the shower.

"What do you mean we?" she asks behind me.

I expected her question, so I don't even break stride or turn around when I answer. "Exactly what I said, babe. We're going to work. Together." I'm not letting her out of my sight, and it has absolutely nothing to do with her sister. Millie is mine, and until she is aware of that and on board with it, we're sticking together.

Chapter 7

JAKE

IN LESS THAN TWENTY-FOUR HOURS, MILLIE HAS managed to turn my world completely upside down. And sitting in the waiting room of a gynecologist's office, listening to women whisper to Millie through a glass window about their pussy problems, is just the icing on the fucking cake.

For fuck's sake, but I've heard it all today. Pussy problem number one: "Something is coming out down there that isn't supposed to." Pussy problem number two: "Something is stuck up there that shouldn't be." Pussy problem number three: "It smells funny down there."

Yep. I'll never think about a pussy the same way ever again after today. And to think that I thought I'd needed earplugs in the car on the way here when Millie cranked up the radio and let her inner diva fly. No. I need those fuckers now, because I am on the verge of what I like to call a pussy breakdown. I'll probably never recover.

Watching Millie work is the only thing keeping me sane. She is kind, sweet, patient, and attentive to all of her patients. She checks them in. She checks them out. Answers phone calls. Deals with last-minute emergencies. And she always keeps her cool. I could tell right away that she was made to care for others. I wonder why she can't see that that's her gift. She'll make an excellent mother and wife someday. Someday soon, hopefully.

The only thing that really bothers me is the doctor she works for. Every chance he gets, he makes eyes at or flirts with my girl. Fucking pussy doctor—creepy fucker. I could only hear half of what he was saying to her from the waiting room, where she demanded I stay the entirety of the day, but I can tell he wants her. I'm not havin' that shit.

It's almost quitting time, and after eight hours of this, I am more than ready to get out of here and get Tillie so that I can spend the rest of the night making love to Millie. I'm checking the clock over the glass window one more time when I see creepy pussy doctor talking to my girl again. He's leaning in too close to her for his own good, and I can see, even from here, that he is trying to get a look down her adorable puppy dog scrubs. I'm out of my seat and pushing through the door to get to the back office before you can say vagina.

I make it to Millie's desk just in time to hear the good doctor ask, "When are you singing, Millie? I've been dying to come out and see you again."

He'll be dying, all right.

Millie finally spots me and shrieks, "Jake! You cannot be back here. I already told you that. What are you doing?"

I stand behind her and rest my hands on her shoulders, giving Doc the best don't-fuck-with-my-girl look I can conjure up. He makes a quick escape, and I feel the last of my patience snap.

Grabbing Millie's wrist and pulling her out of her chair, I snap out, "Bathroom?" I'm so damn angry. I need to make sure she understands she's mine. I can't wait another minute.

"Two doors down on the right," she says, nodding in the general direction.

I drag her down the hallway toward the bathroom.

"Jake, let me go! I am not going to the bathroom with you."

Wrong. I close the bathroom door behind us and turn the light on.

"Jake, we shouldn't be in here. I could get in trouble. This is highly inappropriate." Millie has her hands held out in front of her, warding me off and backing up toward the sink.

Highly inappropriate. I grin. Fuck, she's cute. When her back hits the sink, I can't help but chuckle. I feel like the cat that ate the damn canary. She's right where I want her. Well, almost.

"Turn around and put your hands on the sink, darlin'," I breathe across her lips.

Millie looks confused for a minute, and then I see realization dawn in her eyes.

"Jake, if you think for one minute—" she starts, but I spin her around and grab her wrists.

I place her hands on either side of the sink and press my front to her back. She shivers against me and lets out a small whimper, letting me know she wants this as much as I do.

I let her wrists go and rub my hands up her arms to her shoulders and then down her body to the bottom of her scrub top. "Now, be a good girl and keep your hands right where they are and I'll make you feel good. I promise," I whisper into that sweet-smelling spot between her neck and her shoulder. I pepper the side of her neck with openmouthed kisses, tasting her everywhere my mouth can reach while easing her shirt up with my hands.

I watch her in the mirror. Her head falls to the side to give me better access to her neck. Her mouth is slightly open in ecstasy. Her chest is rising and falling with deep breaths. I pull down the cups of her bra under her breasts and use both of my hands to knead and pinch her nipples. Fuck, she looks filthy dirty in her work clothes with my tanned, rough hands all over her silky, smooth skin. My dick is painfully hard, but I'm enjoying the view too much to stop and do anything about it right now. I only speak when I see her eyes fall closed in the mirror.

"Uh-uh, baby. Open those eyes. I want you to see who's playing with your magnificent tits. I want you to understand who owns this gorgeous body," I say, giving both of her nipples a hard pull at the same time.

She opens her eyes, but I'm not sure if she's seeing anything. Her eyes are so hooded, and they flutter closed every few seconds.

"Keep 'em open, darlin'." I pinch her nipples a little harder, and her eyes pop open wide on a groan.

She's grinding that plump ass hard on my cock, and I'm so turned on that I pray I don't come in my pants like a teenager. After sliding my hands down her sides and into her scrub pants, I ease them down her thighs to her knees. Then I back up a little so I can enjoy the view of her bare ass.

"Jake, we shouldn't... Bad idea... Working..." Her words are jumbled and breathy through her lust-fueled haze.

"We definitely should, Millie," I say, placing my hands on her ass cheeks and pulling them up and apart.

She's so wet that it's dripping down her thighs, and I run one hand farther down and place my middle finger on her clit, giving it a quick stroke. She sucks in a breath and pushes her ass out farther, giving me better access.

"You see, baby. This pussy is mine." I push my fingers inside her, and she groans and leans farther forward on her hands.

I pump my fingers a few more times, feeling how tight and warm she is. She's riding my hand, and I can feel her contracting around my fingers, which tells me she's getting close. I pull my fingers from her pussy and bring them to her mouth.

"Suck," I order.

I watch defiance cross her features in the mirror, but eventually, lust wins out and she gives in, taking my fingers into her mouth and sucking them clean.

"That's right, baby. This mouth is mine, too. All of your sweet self is mine, Millie. Do you understand?" I ask, bringing my hand back down to her ass and running my finger around her anus. "Even this will eventually be mine." I continue rubbing her puckered hole.

"Please, Jake, please," Millie begs, pushing back against my hand.

God, I could fuck her right now against the sink in her office bathroom with her scrubs around her ankles. But she is a virgin and I don't want her first time to be here—like this. It needs to be at home, in our bed, where I can properly make love to her.

"Tell me you understand, Millie. Tell me you

understand that you're mine," I say, using one hand to pop the button on my jeans and drag my cock out while moving my other hand down to stroke her clit.

One flick of my finger and my girl is yelling out, "Yes, please! I'm yours! Just make me come. Please make me come now."

I furiously rub her pussy and plunge my fingers deep inside her while pumping my cock in my other hand. Fuck, this feels amazing, and I need for her to come soon. I could go any minute.

Millie rides my hand like a champ, but when her eyes catch sight of my own hand stroking my cock in the mirror, it sets her off like the Fourth of July. She trembles against my hand on a long, "Jakeee," while I shoot ribbons and ribbons of come all over her ass.

Breathing hard, I use both hands to rub my come into the globes of her ass, marking her in the only way I know how right now. "You are mine, darlin'. You aren't singing for anyone but me. You don't let anyone put their hands on you but me. Especially not Doctor Dickface, you feel me?" I growl out.

"Yeah, Jake. I think I got the memo, honey," she says, slumped over the sink. She sounds out of breath and exhausted.

"Good. Job done," I reply, lifting her sagging body, pulling her pants back up around her waist, and straightening her bra and her top.

Chapter 8

MILLIE

"Before we get home and I remove these scrubs from your body and finally fill you with my cock, we have to deal with your shifty sister," Jake says from the driver's seat of his giant SUV. "It's time to call her. I want us to put this mess behind us and move forward."

I have been dreading this moment. This is when the fun ends and reality kicks in. Once he has Tillie, there's no reason to keep me in his house, his bed, or his life. Can I just resume my life pretending that everything with Jake didn't happen? Will I be happy singing at Bill's and going home to an empty apartment? Knowing the pleasure and pure happiness I get when I am with this pushy—albeit sexy—alpha man but never having it again?

No. This is not the end. I must find a way to stick around long enough for him fall for my crazy, quirky, but surely loveable self.

"Sure, babe. Let me shoot Hannah a quick text first. I need to let her know our weekly Monday 'movies and Mexican' standing date is canceled. Then I'll call Tillie and we can get it all figured out," I explain to him. I hate that I am lying, but it's for a good reason. I want long term with Jake. This is all just a means to an end.

After grabbing my phone off the top of my purse on the floorboard, I discreetly pull up the last text I had with my sister and type out a message using the system we established when we were younger. We were never super close, but back then, we only had each other to count on. When your dad constantly has his hand in several different cons, you make sure you have a plan for when things go south.

CODE RED

I can only hope she doesn't have me blocked and remembers the system we developed. I don't have time to give her more details because Jake looks over and smirks at me. If he sees the text, then my efforts were for nothing and he'll figure out that something is up.

I close the messaging app and start to put my phone away. Loudly clearing his throat in a not-so-subtle way, Jake gets my attention. As I look to him, he raises his eyebrows while glancing down at the phone sitting on top of my bag.

"Darlin', you forgettin' somethin'?" he questions.

I know what I must do. This isn't going to just go away tonight.

"No denying this ain't easy on you, but it's time. She's pissed a lot of men off, myself included. We need to bring her in. Maybe then she can get her life straight." He puts a soothing hand on my thigh in an attempt to reassure me and let me know that everything will work out.

I hope he's right.

I know that what he is saying is true, and at some point, I'm going to have to find a way to get her to him. Still, I need some more time alone with Jake before we have to figure out what this is without the Tillie drama holding us together. I have an apartment, a goal, a life. But, right now, while sitting next to him, I don't care about any of it. I decide to do the only thing that makes sense. I grab my cell and hit dial on the top name.

Ring, Ring, Ring.

Yes! It's going to go to voice mail. This is all gonna be easy-peasy.

"Holla, my fellow whore!" *a* way-too-excited Hannah answers, blowing my plans of leaving a voice mail and avoiding the Tillie issue for another day. "You still with Muscles? I need deets!"

Fuck! "Tillie. It's me," I say in the stiffest voice possible, attempting to get across to my friend what is going on while not blowing my cover with Jake. "We need to talk."

"Oh, are we playing this game?" Hannah says with a giggle, which tells me she isn't going to make this easy for me.

"Come to my boyfriend's house tonight," I spurt out, unable to even register that I just called Jake my boyfriend. Hopefully, he didn't notice. "I'll make dinner and we'll talk everything out. Seven p.m. Davies Drive. Second house on the left."

"Is that where all the sex is happening? I'm not down with the group stuff, Mil. I thought we've been over this. I like all the attention on me," she jokingly tells me, holding in her fit of laughter.

I can't let her make me crack. If I laugh, Jake will figure out that this call is not on the up-and-up.

"See you then," I reply while holding in my giggle. Then I hang up the phone and look over to a skeptical Jake.

Nodding, I reassure him she is coming later and she thinks we are going to be hashing out the whole "stealing my crutches and disappearing" thing.

I'm relieved when we arrive back at Jake's house. I hate lying to him, but I need more time. I climb out of the SUV and start to grab the couple of bags full of my things we got from my place before work from the back. It feels like I'm moving in, which makes me feel a bit giddy, but my brain knows that this is just a temporary arrangement.

"I got that, darlin'. Why don't you go grab a hot shower? I'll get this stuff inside and pull some steaks out to throw on the grill for dinner later," Jake says in his smooth, deep voice before placing a kiss on my forehead.

He carries my overnight bags into his bedroom. It's funny how fast his space already feels like home. After gathering my pajamas, I go to the hall bathroom and make quick work of turning the shower to scorching hot, undressing, and climbing in. This past day has been a lot to take in, and I find myself lost in thought. Before I can fully comprehend what is happening, the curtain is yanked back and a completely naked Jake stands in front me.

"Couldn't take one more second thinkin' of you in here, soaking wet and buck-ass naked. Couldn't wait one more minute to have you. Need to feel you again. Need to taste you again. And fuck if I don't desperately need to finally make you mine," Jake says, climbing in behind me, his words melting my heart.

Which is now racing after the sight of Jake naked.

I feel his massive erection pressed between us as he rubs his hands down my sides. He leans around me to grab the shampoo bottle and pours a small amount into his palm.

With the gentlest of touches, he lathers up my hair. My hormones are in overdrive from his proximity and his touch.

"Turn around," he instructs. "I'm gonna get you clean then take you in our bedroom and dirty you back up."

Unable to do anything but what he asks, I turn toward him and lean my head back, letting the water rinse my hair out and cascade down my back. This moment between us is calmer, softer than any before. Jake washing my hair is so intimate that I should feel shy and reserved, being so innocent, but the way he looks at me like I am the most beautiful woman he has ever seen only seems to energize me. I want more with this man and, at least for now, he wants more from me, too.

His hands leave my hair and cup my face, forcing me to lift my head toward his. He leans in and places the softest of kisses on my lips, causing a small moan to escape my mouth. He takes the opportunity to deepen the kiss, coaxing my tongue out to come and play with his.

Several minutes pass before I finally break the kiss and look in his eyes. They are full of desire and lust. I reach between us and wrap my small hand around his thick cock.

"FUCK!" Jake lets out a loud groan as I guide my hand down his length and back up.

With my thumb, I rub over the small amount of liquid on the tip, making him emit yet another groan. Spurred on by his reaction, I start slowly pumping my hand up and down, squeezing the base each time I reach the end. I don't know what I am doing, but the look on his face and the sounds coming from his mouth tell me I am not doing it wrong.

He drops his head back and closes his eyes. I can tell he

is getting close to coming. Watching him let go in my hands turns me on. I clench my thighs together, needing some sort of friction on my clit. I'm so worked up that I could fall apart from just watching him get off.

Thud. Thud.

A loud banging at the door interrupts the moment.

"Fuck," Jake barks out, pulling away from my greedy hand.

I whimper, upset from not seeing him finish. I desperately wanted to see him come all over my stomach.

Thud. Thud.

We hear the noise from the front door again. It doesn't sound like a normal knock, but instead like something ramming into it. *UGH.* I wish something was ramming into me. But that moment is gone. Horny Jake has left the building, replaced by angry-to-have-been-interrupted Jake.

"Stay here," he demands, obviously agitated. He exits the shower and tugs his jeans up his wet body. He stalks out of the bathroom, heading for the front of the house.

I've never been the best at following orders. I wrap my body in Jake's oversized robe and tie it tight. I follow him to the front of the house, eager to see what all the commotion is. I hope the problem can be solved fast so we can resume shower time.

When I turn the corner, Jake has my sister pushed face-first against the wall next to the door, rubbing his hands up and down her body. It reminds me of what happened between us just a day ago, and I hate seeing him up so close to her, even though he is just doing his job.

"Jake!" I yell at him as he releases her but still uses his imposing body to block the exit.

With his arms crossed over his impeccable, still naked chest and a scowl on his face, he looks between the two of us. He is obviously trying to make sense of the situation unfolding.

"Millie! Why are you and Mr.-Wannabe-Cop here all wet and looking like I interrupted some sexy shower time?" Tillie questions me, looking slightly annoyed.

"'Cause you did," Jake answers for me. "But this works, too. I can get you to Manny. Then me and my girl can pick up where we left off." He pauses while staring Tillie down. "*Without* anymore interruptions."

"I said Code Red," I reply, ignoring Jake's response.

"Red means 'I've been kidnapped. Come fast,' right?" she asks while rubbing her sore arm. Trying to break the door down with her small frame might not have been her best decision.

"Tillie! That's Code Blue! Code Red was 'I've been kidnapped, but it's all good and I think I want to stay.' I'm not leaving here. He has all the orgasms," I state, unable to believe she could have gotten it all so wrong.

For someone who looks identical to me, she couldn't be more different. There is no one who can get me to go from zero to sixty like Tillie. Well, *almost* no one.

I hear Jake chuckle, but I cannot focus on him right now. I'm in a fit of rage at my sister, who once again is messing everything up. I do not have time to deal with him laughing at me. I am pissed.

"And where did you get that car?" I question, pointing over Jake's shoulder, out the open door, to a classic, pale-blue Oldsmobile. "I know it's not yours."

"Borrowed it from a friend," she replies curtly.

"Yeah, right. A *friend*," I say, rolling my eyes, holding my hands up in air quotes. "Is this the same *friend* you've been staying with down at the Wild Acres Retirement Center? Does your *friend* know you are using him to hide while you skip out on your bail?"

"I can't believe I came here to save you! You are so judgmental. You never try to see anything from my point of view!" Tillie yells back at me.

Jake looks between us, kneading his temples, exasperated from trying to keep up with the conversation between my sister and me. "Ladies!" he interrupts loudly, causing our escalating fight to come to a halt.

We both look at him, waiting to see what he is going to say next.

Chapter 9

JAKE

IT WAS A GODDAMN CODE BLUE, ALL RIGHT. AS IN BLUE
balls. Fucking Tillie. This woman is turning out to be the
bane of my very existence. Not only has she had me chasing
her crazy ass around town for weeks, but now, she just tried
to break my door down about two seconds before I was
going to come all over her sister's hands. And stomach. And
breasts. Fuck. Me. Somehow, I think my dick just got
harder, and I didn't even think that was possible. I adjust my
wet, aching cock with my hand and get back to the two
deranged women in my living room.

"I don't even want to know why the hell you two have
codes for being kidnapped." I shake my head and point my
finger at Tillie. "Or why in God's name you are breaking
into *my* house." I point to myself now. "You know, the man
who has been trying to arrest you for weeks now. I feel like
I'm on some kind of fucked-up show and cameras are going
to pop out any minute, letting me know I'm being fucking
Punk'd."

I stare hard at both ladies, letting them know I mean
business. I've had it up to my damn eyeballs with these two.

Millie chews on her lips and looks a little ashamed, but not Tillie. She's taking me in. Her eyes ghost over my entire body before zeroing in on my rock-hard cock, which is tenting my tight, wet jeans. She crosses her arms over her chest and raises an eyebrow, nudging Millie with her shoulder.

"You sure you want your first go to be with that python?" She nods to my dick with a smirk.

Millie gasps and turns toward her sister. "Do not even, Tillie. Do not talk about Jake Blackwood's junk! Just don't!"

"Jake *Blackwood*?" Tillie laughs loudly. "And here I thought for sure y'all'd be on a first-name basis and all after what I just witnessed."

I back up because I can see it coming from a mile away.

"Do not start your shit, Tillie." Millie lunges at her, taking her to the floor in what would under normal circumstances be damn good entertainment, but not today.

Today, I'm at my wit's end.

"Dear God," I rumble under my breath and take a seat on the couch. I look up at the ceiling and pray for patience. Because I realize I am falling in love with one of those crazy women on the floor. I want to keep her. I want to protect her. I want to love her. And knowing all of that means knowing I am keeping and protecting and loving all of that crazy, too.

A crashing lamp brings me out of my thoughts and back to the twins wrestling almost underneath my coffee table. Millie has Tillie pinned down with a forearm across her throat, and I feel a little pride at how tough my girl is. And that's when I realize I've officially lost my mind, too.

"You stole my crutches, Till! Who in the hell does that?

What is wrong with you?" she yells an inch from her sister's face.

Tillie rolls her until they are out from under the table. Then she straddles Millie, holding her arms down. She sits up and looks down at her. "It was for your own damn good!" she yells back.

"My own damn good? My own good? How can stealing a crippled girl's crutches be for her own good?" Millie screams at the top of her lungs.

And, if I thought they were fighting before, I was wrong.

There's rolling, kicking, punching, and hair-pulling, and for a while, I just watch. But, when they break another lamp, I decide to intervene. These crazy fools are breaking all of my shit.

I pull the girls apart and place my body between them, but not before Millie accidentally nails me in the mouth with her shin. "Fuck," I mutter, wiping the blood off my lip and sitting back.

"Oh, Jake, I'm so sorry, honey. I was caught up. I didn't mean to hurt you." She comes toward my face in that way chicks do when they want to check you over.

But I'm in no mood to be babied. I'm downright pissed. They've denied me orgasms. They've trashed my living room. They've broken my shit. And, now, I have a busted lip.

"Sit! Now!" I roar at both of them.

Both of their asses hit the floor with the quickness, and I want to cheer in victory. I will tame this crazy if it kills me. And it might.

I need to get Tillie gone, which means taking her in now, so that I can get back to my girl. I can only deal with one insane chick at a time, and Millie is mine, so the decision is simple.

"Tillie." I look at her. "I'm going to put you in my car right now and I'm takin' you down to the county jail. And you are going to be a good girl and not fight me. Understand?"

The twins answer almost simultaneously.

"But she's my sister," Millie says quietly.

"But I'm her sister!" Tillie cries out.

They both wear the same look of despair. Both of their icy-blue eyes are turned down. Both of their pretty, pink mouths are poked out in a pout. And I realize right away I can't do this. Millie loves Tillie. No matter what a thieving lunatic she might be. And I love Millie. I can't believe I've been chasing this chick around for weeks and I don't even get to take her in. I am going to get so much shit at work. I realize I would do anything for Millie. But I still can't let Tillie just get away. She needs to get her shit together. Her sister needs her. And I want Millie happy.

A look I know all too well crosses Millie's features. Trouble. "Tillie needs to use the bathroom." She nudges her sister.

"I do?" Tillie asks, looking at Millie.

Millie gives her a hard stare.

"Why, yes, I do," she says, grinning.

I can't help but shake my head at their antics. "Go on, then," I grumble out at them. "I gotta make a call before I take you in anyhow."

They dart out of the room like their asses are on fire, and I find my cell phone on the kitchen counter. I put in a call to my street cop friend, Nathan Trent.

"Trent," he says, answering the phone.

"Hey, man. I have a huge favor," I say into the phone, and it is huge because the lady currently climbing out of my bathroom window is a damn psychopath.

I feel a little bad for pawning her off on Trent, but still, I find myself letting out a relieved sigh. She's someone else's problem now. Hopefully.

"Shoot," Trent says. He is always straight to the point, and it is one of the reasons I get along with him so well.

"I'm ninety-nine percent sure that Tillie Coletrain is sneaking out of my bathroom window right now. Could you come by and pick her up and take her in?" I let out another relieved sigh.

He chuckles. "How come you're letting her climb out the window?"

I pinch the bridge of my nose and tell him the only reason that comes to mind. "Millie."

Chapter 10

MILLIE

I OPEN THE BATHROOM DOOR JUST ENOUGH TO squeeze my body out and then close the door behind me. Jake is going to be pissed when he realizes Tillie is gone, but she's my sister. I couldn't just let my man arrest her. We may not be close, but I remember the pain of being abandoned after my momma left us. I won't do that do her.

"Where's Tillie?" Jake asks, startling me.

"Umm . . ." I stammer out, trying to buy time. "She's having female problems."

I have no idea why I gave an excuse instead of just telling him she's gone. He's going to find out. I just need a minute to come up with something.

"What a coincidence. I'm havin' *female* problems, too," he says, shaking his head side to side. "Darlin', y'all ain't exactly good at being subtle. She's your sister. It was important to you I not take her in, and I plan on being with you for a long time. Didn't feel like havin' you mad at me when we're together. Plus, as much as I want you in my life, and trust me I do, I also really want to get my cock in your sweet pussy. Want it all from you.

Everything. In my life *and* in my bed. Didn't seem like that would be happening if I left here to take your sister to jail."

I'm in love with this man. It only took a day, but he is the only one for me. He's ungodly sexy, protective, possessive, and desperate for me. I've never cared what others around me thought of me, but knowing that Jake thinks I'm perfect has me eager and excited for more.

Everything about the way he's looking at me lets me know he desires me. His eyes are dark and hooded, and his voice has gotten huskier. This man wants me. And *God* do I want him.

"Take me to bed, Jake," I rasp out, my heart beating wildly.

We barely make it into the room before he has me pressed up against the wall. Leaning his head down, he kisses me, his tongue teasing the seam of my lips. When I part them, he takes my mouth in a punishing kiss. He is hungry and frantic.

I'm in a complete daze, so it barely registers when he starts pulling the knot out of the robe tied around my body. I don't even have time to protest. He's still wearing his jeans, while I'm completely bare before him. He palms my breast in his hand and roughly pinches my nipple.

"Jake!" I gasp out, greedy for more.

No more than a moment passes before he takes the same nipple in his mouth, soothing the pain away. He has me crazed, hot, and aching. This is a whole new Millie. A me that exists only for Jake.

"You ready for this, babe?" he asks me. He releases my breast from the delicious heat of his mouth and starts to unsnap the button on his jeans. "Once I'm finally inside you, you're mine. There's no goin' back from here."

"Yes," I cry on a breath, letting my robe fall from my shoulders and puddle on the floor. "I want this. I want you. I want *us*." And I do. I want him like my next breath. I step away from him and lie down on the bed, an invitation for him to join me.

A wicked smile crosses his face as his hooded eyes take in my naked body. He removes his pants, and his gorgeous cock springs free. Hard and long, it smacks him in the stomach before he takes it in his hand and gives it a firm tug. I lie frozen on the bed, watching him touch himself. I have never felt anything this erotic. I'm torn between needing to watch him and needing him to touch me.

"Been hard all day thinkin' about your taste, the way you feel in my hands, the desire on your face while you come. Touching you at work and feeling your hand in the shower did nothing to ease this ache." His voice is rough and his eyes never leave me while he continues to slowly stroke himself. "Not gonna wear a condom. Want you bare. We're forever, and nothing will be between us."

"Jake, I could get pregnant," I soberly explain. I want that, too. I want to feel *all* of him, but I don't want him to feel obligated to me because of a baby.

"Darlin', we've been over this. I know where babies come from, and honestly, the thought of you pregnant only gets me harder. Nothing would make me happier than having *my* baby inside you. Just thinking about you swollen with my child makes me fuckin' crazy with lust."

His words send a jolt of excitement through me. I reach up for him and pull his body closer to mine.

His hungry eyes take me in while he climbs down the bed and throws my legs over his shoulders. With no hesitation, he starts to tease my clit, rotating between licking and sucking. My back arches off the bed, and a throbbing pulse deep within me starts to spread. My head thrashes side to side and my hands gather fists full of sheets as my orgasm builds. I close my eyes and erupt, too lost in the feel of him ravaging me like a man starved.

Jake moves up my body, and I know what's next. He slides the head of his cock through my wetness several times, coating it with my juices, making sure I'm ready for him. With a gentle thrust, he pushes in and breaks through my barrier. I cry out, equal parts pleasure and pain pinching at my core. Jake holds completely still, letting the pain ease and allowing my body to get used to the blissful fullness I'm feeling. It is unparalleled, and with him rooted deep inside me, I know that nothing else could ever feel this good.

"So tight!" Jake grunts. His eyes close as if he is using all of his concentration to hold still.

I want him to move. Watching him try to hold off is hypnotic. My pussy clenches firmly around him, and I reassure him that I'm okay. I am more than okay. Everything in me is throbbing, and with just him holding still inside me, I'm already close to another orgasm.

"Move. Jake, I need you to move," I rasp out, desperate for more.

Slowly, he begins to glide in and out of me—stroking every nerve along the way. My body's writhing beneath him, and with every controlled thrust, I fall apart a little bit more. The pleasure building is unlike anything I've ever experienced. I can tell that Jake is holding back, trying to be careful, but he's slowly losing the battle with every moan that escapes my mouth. I squeeze him tighter and push my body up toward his, letting him know I'm ready to take everything he has to give.

"Knowin' I'm the only man to ever be here, that will ever be here, is the best feelin' in the fucking world. All this beauty," he calmly proclaims. He pulls out until only the tip remains inside me. "Just for me." And, with no more hesitation, he dives into me in one quick hard thrust.

"Yours. Only ever yours!" I yell out, my orgasm taking over my body.

Feeling me come must set something off inside him, because before I can finish, he is pounding into me like a man on a mission. Frenzied and determined, Jake takes me with raw abandon, and as he comes, it's my name on his lips.

Slowly pulling out of me, Jake sits up at my knees and looks down at my sweaty, limp, content body. He rubs two of his fingers through my folds, spreading the come leaking out until it coats me.

"You covered in me is the hottest thing I've ever seen, and if I wasn't worried about you bein' sore tomorrow, I could take you all over again right now," he says as he stops touching me and leaves the bed. "I'll be right back," he tells me. He leaves the room but returns just seconds later with a washcloth.

I reach for it, and he pushes my hands away.

"Let me," he states firmly. He wipes me clean and tosses the washcloth on the floor with the robe.

I'm starting to think Jake would be willing to take care of almost anything for me.

"I know the way you helped your sister out tonight was because you love her. I might not fully understand y'all's relationship, but I get it," he explains as he climbs into bed next to me, pulling the sheet up, covering our naked bodies. "Just know, the next time shit goes down and you're lying to me, I'm goin' to spank that sexy, plump ass of yours while I fuck you from behind so I can see my handprint there the whole time. And trust me, darlin'. I'm gonna enjoy every second of it."

I should not be turned on by what he is promising. He's bossy and demanding. Normally, I would fight back if anyone talked to me like that. Yet, right now, hearing him say these deliciously sexy words, I find not only am I not mad, but I'm incredibly turned on. I just don't know if my body could handle anymore.

"Okay, Jake Blackwood," I sigh, completely sated and unable to fight him. "We can make that a plan for another day."

Completely exhausted from this life-changing day, I'm unable to keep my eyes open for a moment more. I fall asleep with Jake's arms around me and his warm breath on my neck.

Chapter 11

JAKE

I have come to the conclusion that the twins are fucking ninjas. The empty spot next to me in bed is all the proof I need. I look at the clock on the bedside table. It's only three in the morning. Where the hell is Millie, and why didn't I hear her getting out of bed? Because—ninjas. All of my law enforcement training and I can't even keep up with my girlfriend.

Girlfriend? God, what in the hell is wrong me? I've got it bad for this woman. She's got me doing all kinds of crazy shit—kidnapping her and letting her sister go. I'm out of my damn mind, and I know why. Because I love this woman. It's only been a day and she has me tied up in knots. I can't believe I've fallen so hard and so fast.

I rub my hand over the spot next to me. It's still warm, so I know she isn't far. I get up quietly and slip on some sweatpants. My dick's already hard again, and I'm ready for round two. Last night was the best sex of my entire life. Millie's silky, tight, wet pussy milking my cock is the best feeling I've ever experienced. I want her again. Now. And she isn't in bed where she is supposed to be. I feel my temper climb.

I search my bathroom and my closet first and then make my way around my house on stealthy feet. I don't want to scare her even though I want to spank her never-listening ass. I search the kitchen and the living room and feel my anger fading. Because, now, I'm freaking the hell out. Did she leave? How could she leave? Surely, she knows how I feel about her. I've made it fucking obvious. My pulse skyrockets, and I feel sick. Panic takes hold as I run back into the bedroom and then search every room in the house again.

I hear something in the living room, so I stop and try to calm my breathing. Whispering. Someone is whispering, and it sounds like it's coming from the coat closet. I walk closer and lean my head gently to the door.

"Call me back when you get this. Please. I'm worried."

I hear a rushed whisper and then the beep of a cell call ending.

This woman drives me up the damn wall. I take a deep breath, garnering all of my patience, and open the door to the closet. Millie is sitting in the corner of the closet in the dark, only the small cell phone screen lighting her shocked face.

She lets out a small squeak that sounds something like, "Jake!"

I shake my head at her batshit crazy. I don't know how, but she keeps managing to surprise me. You'd think, by now, I'd expect anything, but no, I'm still shocked every time she pulls one of her stunts.

"Hi," she says sweetly from underneath about five giant men's coats hanging above her. "What's up?" she asks like she's not sitting in the bottom of a coat closet in my living room at three in the morning.

"Hey, Millie. Oh, nothing," I say back like I'm not wondering what in the ever-loving hell is going on right now.

I have a temper, I know. And I'm at my wit's end with this woman. She tries my patience almost as much as she makes my dick hard, and most of the time, I kinda like it. But not right now. Not when I'm supposed to be sleeping and not when my cock could be buried in her sweet pussy.

I roll my neck around a couple of times and breathe in and out, taking a few calming breaths. Millie watches like a hawk. I can feel her trying to anticipate my next move.

"Get out of the damn closet, Millie," I growl out to the ceiling.

"Jake, I was just—" she starts, but I cut her off.

"Just what, Millie?" My head snaps down, and my eyes meet hers. I run a hand through my hair. "Just what good excuse do you have for hiding in my coat closet in the middle of the fucking night?" I let out a sarcastic chuckle. "Please enlighten me. I can't wait to hear what you come up with." I stare her down, waiting on an answer.

She's still just hiding in that damn closet, probably terrified to come out. I can tell by the way her eyes dart around nervously and she picks at my shirt that this is going to be good. I can hardly wait.

I cross my arms over my chest and stare down at her. "Well?"

She looks at me like *I* did something wrong. I try to keep from smiling because she is being cute, but I'm still mad as hell.

"I was hungry, Jake. Is it against the law to order Chinese food past whatever time you deem it appropriate?" she barks at me.

Chinese food, my ass. I caught the last part of that conversation. She is lying to me again, and I warned her what would happen if she lied to me. I think argumentative Millie is fucking cute. Sneaky Millie is adorable. But lying Millie can take a fucking hike. I don't like that shit, and I won't stand for it from the woman I love.

I bend down and roughly grab her arm, dragging her from the closet. "I told you not to fucking lie to me, Millie. I warned you about that shit. I'll put up with a lot from you because you've come to mean a great deal to me in the last day, but not this. Not the lying. You understand?" I demand, dragging her down the hallway.

"Jake, I wasn't—"

But I stop her before she can tell me another lie. She's only making this harder for herself.

"Think before you spout another untruth, Millie, because I am at my wit's end with you right now. You feel me?" I snap out. I throw her on the bed and pull my T-shirt off her naked body.

She's gripping the cell phone in her hand like it's her lifeline.

I feel murderous that she is hiding things from me. "Give me the phone. Now."

She sits up and puts her arms over her breasts, shielding

her body from me. And, if I thought I was mad before, I'm enraged now.

"You did not just throw me on this bed like a rag doll, Jake Blackwood!" She holds the phone up like it's a goddamn trophy. "And you are never getting this. Ever!" she shouts. "It's mine and you can't have it!"

I almost laugh at the ridiculousness of the situation, because after all, I am the sane one here. But, right before I break into laughter, Millie tucks and rolls to her stomach, keeping the phone gripped tight in both hands, hidden beneath her torso. I'd be mad at this, but it places her face in the sheets and her juicy ass right in the air for the taking. After taking my sweatpants off, I climb into bed and curl the front of my body over the back of hers.

My lips are next to her ear when I whisper, "I've got you right where I want you now. I told you what would happen if you lied to me." I feel her body stiffen at my words, and I can't help the smirk on my face.

Leaning back, I look down at Millie. She's on her knees, her ass in the air, and her face to the mattress. Fuck. It's the sexiest thing I've ever seen in my life. I'm so turned on that I'm not even mad anymore, but she has a lesson to learn and I am all too happy to give it. My cock is, too, if the precum leaking from the head of it is any indication.

I rub my palm over one of her ass cheeks while slowly stroking my cock. God. I could come like this. Just stroking myself and watching her. I could come all over her ass and back and rub it all in so she'd remember who she belonged to. So she'd never get any ideas about lying to me again. This isn't about what I want though. This is about teaching Millie.

I stop stroking myself and place both hands on her ass cheeks, spreading them wide so I can see all the way down the crease of her bottom to the cream dripping from her pussy below.

"You're soaking wet, baby. You want my cock, don't you?" I lean forward over her body and rub the head of my dick through her dripping heat. It feels good, and I'm almost tempted to give her what she wants—slide right in there.

It takes some willpower, but I pull back and bring my right hand down on her ass cheek. Millie jolts forward and grunts. The handprint on her ass sends my lust higher, so I bring my hand down on her other ass cheek hard. She rocks back into me and groans low in her throat. Fuck, she is loving this.

"Fuck, your cunt is dripping, baby. You like it when I spank you, don't you?" I say, rubbing my hands over her ass, soothing the burn.

She tries to move her arms and her torso up, but I push her back down and hold her to the mattress.

"Uh-uh, darlin'. You stay right where you are and be a good girl." I rub my hand down her spine.

I swear I hear her fucking purr.

"That's right, baby. You're a good girl." I want to reward her for being so compliant. I bring my hand down hard on her bottom again and again. If I had known a good spanking would have calmed her ass down, I'd have started with that. "Want me to fuck that pussy or eat it? Your choice, babe," I groan out, rubbing my dick through her wet folds.

"Please fuck me, Jake. Please," Millie begs, pushing her ass back against me.

God, I want her so bad and she looks so fucking hot right now.

I line up my cock with her sweet hole and push all the way in—hard. Millie makes a loud keening sound, and for a second, I'm worried I hurt her.

But then she pushes back against me and yells, "I said fuck me, Jake! Now."

Spreading her ass cheeks wide with my hands, I watch my cock take her pussy hard. Her wetness coats my cock, and I pause, trying to rein my orgasm in. I'm not ready to come yet, but the sight of her taking me is about to send me over the edge. Millie apparently doesn't' want me to stop, because she pushes back against me and takes my cock all the way to the root. She moves forward, and it slides all the way out to the tip before she slams back and takes me all the way in again.

"Yeah. That's it, baby. Ride that cock. Take it all," I growl out, holding her hips and keeping her spread open so I can see everything. "I wish you could see your tight cunt taking me. It's the sexiest fucking thing I've ever seen in my life."

She groans, and I know that my dirty talk makes her crazy with lust.

"Fuck, Jake. I'm going to come," Millie says breathlessly, slamming back against me one final time.

Her pussy spasms around me, milking my cock and pushing me over the edge, too. "Fuck, baby. You're so good, milking my cock like that," I say, curling myself around her.

I pull her onto her side with me, spooning her so that I can make sure my dick stays deep in that pussy. I don't want any of me leaking out of her. I need to make sure not a drop escapes. I want her pregnant now. The thought of her swollen with my child—her breasts big and heavy—makes me content.

So content that I fall right off to sleep.

Chapter 12

MILLIE

I wake with the sun bursting through the windows and Jake's cock nestled between my ass cheeks. I desperately want to roll over, climb the mountain of a man lying next to me, and go for a ride, but my stomach is growling and, when Jake wakes, he'll be starved. Neither of us had dinner, opting instead to spend our time wrapped around each other. After all the energy we exerted last night, I need to refuel, and I can only imagine that a man like Jake needs sustenance, too.

After slipping out of bed, I quietly rummage through my bag, looking for a clean pair of panties to slip on under the T-shirt of Jake's I grabbed from the floor. I start to worry what will happen when he wakes and I'm not there. Will he hunt me down and show me a repeat of last night? While the dampness in my fresh panties tells me I'm not opposed to the idea, we both need to eat first. Hopefully, waking up to a home-cooked breakfast will keep him calm.

I tiptoe out of the room and make my way to the kitchen. I need to see what kind of supplies I'm working with. Opening the fridge, I'm excited to find it stocked full, so I grab everything I need for my famous French toast. Okay, it's only famous with Hannah. And I only say it's famous because she demands I make it every weekend when she is hungover, recovering from her questionable decisions.

I'm pulling the last piece off the stove when Jake saunters into the room in just a pair of gray sweats. Lord help me! Jake wore jeans amazingly well, but the sight of him in those sweats has me ready to ditch breakfast and climb back in bed with him. A rumble from my stomach reminds me why it's not a good plan right now.

"Sit," I say, motioning toward the breakfast bar. "I made breakfast. We never did get a chance to eat last night."

"Yeah, that's the strange thing about lying about ordering Chinese food." He smirks at me, a gleam in his eye. "Somehow, it never comes. Imagine that."

I glare at him as I set a plate in front of him. I know he is picking on me. However, I also remember how he was pissed at me for lying to him. I'm sure, in his job, people are constantly lying and scheming to get away. I shouldn't have treated him like the criminals he chases do. Still, I needed to make sure Tillie is okay. We might not always see eye to eye, but she is my sister and I'm worried about her. She has been more distant lately and making even more bad decisions than normal.

"About that . . ." I start, unsure how to continue the conversation without pissing Jake off.

"Eat, darlin'," he says. "This food is fuckin' delicious, and we got a lot to go over today. Eat. Then we talk. Then, finally, I'm gonna fuck you against this counter with you in *my* shirt."

"Jake! You know I have work today. I've only got an hour to get ready and be there."

"Here's the deal, darlin'. You need to eat. It's not sitting right with me that I let you go too long without a meal. You need the energy, I'm fuckin' starved, and you made me breakfast which smells abso-fuckin-lutely delicious," he declares before he takes a large bite of the French toast and hums out his approval. After swallowing and grabbing his cup of coffee I set out for him, he continues to inform me how it is all going down.

"First, we're gonna eat. Then we gotta talk about your sister. Once we get that out of the way, we're gonna double-task," he declares, smiling ear to ear.

"Double-task?" I ask, very curious as to what he means.

"Yeah, babe. You're gonna get ready for work by takin' a shower with me while I fuck you. This way, you won't be too late. Now, though," he says, using his fork to point at my plate. "Eat."

He clears his plate, and once I finish, he grabs both plates and heads toward the sink. I follow him and instinctively begin to dry the dishes as he washes. It feels like we're a real couple who've been together for years. Everything with Jake has felt natural.

"Darlin', Tillie's been taken in," he calmly starts to explain as I dry the dishes.

When his words sink in, I throw the towel I'm using on the counter with a huff.

"What the hell, Jake?" I say, stomping my foot as I turn to face him.

"Now, before you go working yourself into a tizzy, give

me a chance to catch you up," he states, rubbing his hands up and down my arms to calm me. "Tillie's in trouble, babe. Not life and death yet, but she's spiraling and it's not getting any better. When we met, I was chasing her for skipping out on her hearing for theft and writing bad checks. I know these seem like small cons, but she's on a path leading to way worse."

I stare at him while he lays all of this on me and let it all sink in. I know that Tillie has to deal with the consequences of her actions. Still, it doesn't lessen the sting of knowing that Jake had a hand in her arrest.

"Despite you constantly telling me y'all aren't close, I could see that her being your sister means a shit-ton to you. I decided almost immediately when she showed up I couldn't take her in. Tillie can't break the law and just get away with it. If we just let her go, she'll inevitably start getting braver and braver, and eventually, she'll get into some real trouble. So, while you were helping her escape, I called my friend Trent. He's a cop. A good one. He picked her up and took her in. He'll make sure she is treated right and gets the help she needs to set her life straight."

I stand silent for a couple of minutes, letting his words sink in. I want to be mad—though, deep down, I know he's right. Tillie doesn't know any other life. Conning is all she has ever known; it's what she had to do to survive. Unlike me, she's never had any other hobbies to drive her away from our father's path. If Jake's friend can help her, then I have to let the hurt go and accept that Jake did this for me.

"Okay, Jake Blackwood. Now, let's go get clean," I reply, shocking him with my compliance.

The way he hesitates and stares back at me proves he was expecting a fight. After a second or two, he realizes there isn't one coming from me. Then he grabs my hand and pulls me down the hall to the bathroom.

An hour and a half later, I'm very full, very clean, very happy, and very, very late. I rush to grab my bag and my keys to head to work. Thankfully, Jake had someone bring my car from Bill's at some point yesterday because he's not planning on chaperoning me at work anymore. I guess, now that he has Tillie in custody, he doesn't need me close every minute of the day.

"Darlin'," Jake calls out to me just as I am opening the door to leave. "When you get home tonight, we need to sit down and discuss us and deal with your things."

Because I'm unable to get Jake's words out of my head, the day drags on and on. I spend the entire day in a trance, worried about tonight. Until he mentioned packing up and going home, the idea of leaving never crossed my mind. Now, it's all I can think about. Luckily, the last few patients canceled and I'm able to leave early. I pull onto Jake's street nervous and on edge. After the time we shared, I thought there was more to us than just a spark of sexual chemistry. Being with him just feels right. In his life, in his house, and in his bed—that's where I belong. I just wish Jake felt the same.

When I near his driveway, the car Tillie borrowed is gone. In its spot is a shiny, silver convertible, the top down. Definitely a chick car. What the hell! A sinking feeling hits my gut. He's not expecting me for another hour for our talk. I park my car a couple of houses down and do my best ninja impersonation as I creep from tree to tree to remain hidden.

I near the front of the house and jump behind the bushes in front of his windows.

"Fuckity fuck, fuck, fuck," I whisper-yell to myself as I peer into the kitchen window.

Jake is embracing a petite brunette woman. Her arms are wrapped tight around him, and he's kissing the top of her head in a way that is too intimate for this to be anything but personal. I have no clue who this woman is or what she means to Jake. I instantly hate her. My heart is breaking as I watch the man I was starting to think of as mine hold another woman.

"Shit," I spurt out just as Jake looks up from the gentle kiss he was giving the woman.

Immediately, he makes eye contact with me as I peer in like a crazed stalker. I always thought, when I would eventually have stalker problems, I would be on the receiving end like Britney, not the one having the cops called on her.

After backing out of the bushes, I run to my car with the quickness I need to get out of here. The tears streaming down my face reaffirm what my heart already knows. I might have only met Jake a couple of days ago, but I'm already in love with him.

"Millie!" Jake yells out at me from the front porch as I near the edge of his yard. "God dammit, darlin', get back here!"

I hear him behind me but ignore him. I don't need him to confess to my face how he's done with me. I pick up my pace, running down the street to where I left my car before my sting operation. I'm close to the car when I trip over my own feet and fall over myself, ripping my pants and skinning my knee. This day could not get any worse. I just need to get home so I can cry and veg out with Hannah. We'll get impossibly drunk while rewatching my old DVR'd episodes of *The X-Factor*. If Britney can't cheer me up, then nothing can.

Chapter 13

JAKE

"I TAKE IT THE GORGEOUS BLONDE CREEPING ON YOU through the window is Millie?" Alex comes up behind me on the porch and rubs my back, offering me a little comfort.

"Listen, honey," I tell Alex. "I gotta go. I know you understand. Stay put. I'll be back soon, and hopefully, I'll have Millie with me so that you guys can get to know each other, okay?"

She gives me a big hug and a kiss on the cheek. "Go get your girl, Boo Bear. I'll be waiting here when you get back," she says, grinning.

Boo Bear. My sister has been calling me that since I was born. She is two years older than I am and the only other woman in my life besides Millie. We are the only family we have because my mom passed away four years ago from a heart attack. Our dad has never been in the picture. We were always there for each other. Which is why, when she showed up at my door today, crying over the latest asshole who was fucking with her heart, I invited her in. I made her lunch and listened. Millie showed up just as I was getting ready to say goodbye to Alex.

Fucking Millie, always ready to run. What she doesn't know is that I'll chase her down anywhere—every day. If it means she is mine, I'll run after her forever.

I jog toward my truck and take a deep breath, trying to calm the banging of my heart. I know what Millie thinks she saw, and the thought of her in pain causes a dull ache to take root behind the hammering in my chest. Fuck, I gotta get to my girl. I have to set things straight like I planned to when she got home from work today.

The few minutes it takes to get to Millie's place are the longest of my life. I am damn near frantic by the time I knock on her door. It's silent and my knocks go unanswered.

"Millie, baby, open the door so we can talk. I can explain," I say as my knocks on the door turn into thundering pounds. I know she is there because I see her car in the parking lot.

When I hear movement on the other side of the door, relief coasts through my body.

"There's nothing to explain, Jake the Snake. Millie isn't home. Get lost," Hannah says from the other side of the door.

Is she fucking kidding me? *Jake the Snake?* And I thought Millie was certifiable. I roll my eyes and breathe in through my nose. I don't want to lose my cool with Hannah. She is Millie's friend, after all, but I don't have time for this. Millie is in pain and only I can set it right.

I bang on the door again. "Hannah, open the goddamn door so I can talk to Millie," I say, trying to keep my voice even.

"Not a chance in hell!" comes from the other side of the door.

Fucking Hannah and her meddling bullshit. I feel my good intentions at remaining calm slip away. My temper and my anger take over.

"Open this fucking door, for fuck's sake, before I knock it down. Right now!" I pound hard on the door.

"Sure, Jake the Snake. Just break down our door like you broke Millie's heart!"

Hannah's words hurt me as much as they piss me the hell off.

I lean forward and drop my forehead to the door with a thud. Then I realize I need to get creative if I want in. Unless I break in. I could, but Millie wouldn't like it if I busted down her door, and I've caused enough problems for her today. I decide it's time to just come clean. You know, the whole "truth will set you free" gig—maybe the truth will get me in.

"I love her," I say quietly to the door, hoping that Hannah can hear me. "I love her so much it hurts. I was going to tell her today. I had plans to do it over a nice meal this evening when she got home. What she thinks she saw just isn't true. I'd never hurt her like that because hurting her hurts me, too. Please, just let me in." I roll my forehead against the door and close my eyes, praying Hannah takes pity on me and lets me in.

The door pops open a couple of inches, and I stand back. Hannah's small, smiling face appears.

"Well, why didn't you start with that, Muscles? She's in her room." Hannah steps back and opens the door wide. She does a grand sweeping motion with her hand, which I assume means to come on in.

My knocks go unanswered for the second time today. I

turn the knob to her door, and surprisingly, it's unlocked, so I go in. I look around the room, searching for her, but her spotless room looks like she hasn't even been here. I search the en suite bathroom and look under the perfectly made bed.

Fuck, where the hell is she? I look around the room one more time, spot her closet in the corner, and feel my heart drop. She's in there. I just know it, and I feel terrible that she is in there, hiding from me again.

I open the door and see a red-faced Millie. Her eyes are swollen, and she has her arms wrapped around her knees. Seeing her curled around herself makes me feel like the most terrible person in the world. She doesn't look surprised to see me, but she doesn't look happy, either. I drop down into the small closet, squeezing my big frame inside across from her. I grab her, pulling her into my lap.

"How did you find me?" she asks through tears, turning her face to look up at me.

"Darlin', haven't you realized by now that I'll find you wherever you go?" I breathe across her lips.

Fuck, she has me tied up in knots right now. My heart is damn near bursting with love for this woman.

Fresh tears fall down her face. She hiccups on a sob, and my stomach turns at her pain.

"But why, Jake. Why? I saw you. I saw you with—"

But I cut her off. "Baby, you saw me with my sister, Alexandra. And she is back at my house, waiting for us. She can't wait to meet the girl stalking me from the bushes," I joke.

"Your sister?" she breathes out like she can't believe it.

The shock on her face makes me chuckle, and I hug her

close to me, breathing in her peppermint scent. I'm sitting in the bottom of a damn closet with my girl, but I don't give a shit where we are as long as we're together.

"I was going to do this tonight when you got home from work, but you foiled my plans, as usual. So I guess I get to do this in the bottom of your small-ass closet." I rest my forehead harder against hers. "Fuck, I love you so much, Millie."

"You love me?" Millie asks, her face full of awe.

"I do. So much. I love your awful singing. I love your ridiculous antics. I love how you love your crazy criminal-ass sister. I love it all, and I want it for always. I don't know what you have in store for me because you always seem to surprise me, but I want those surprises, too," I say, kissing the tip of her nose.

She stays silent. I'm shocked because I don't think my girl has been quiet a day in her life.

"Say something," I demand.

"You love me." She smiles, and I nod. "You really love me," she says again.

I laugh. "How could I not? Everything about you calls to me, Millie," I say in all seriousness.

I keep waiting for her to say it back, but she's just staring at me, her eyes full of her emotion.

"But do you love me?" I finally ask.

"What? Oh my God! Of course I love you." She laughs. "I'm sorry. I'm just so shocked you love me." She smiles and hugs me tight.

"Thank fuck," I mutter, standing up and pulling her up with me. "Now, can we get the fuck outta this closet, pack your shit, and get home?"

"Home?" Millie asks, her face a mask of shock again.

"Yes, darlin'. Home with me. Where you are fucking staying until you do some crazy shit and I have to chase you down again." I chuckle at the thought of chasing her down again. I love that my girl gives me a run for my money.

She smiles and hugs me, pressing her lips to my ear. "The only place I'll be running to, Jake Blackwood, is your bed."

Epilogue

MILLIE
3 YEARS LATER

"GET THERE, DARLIN'," JAKE WHISPERS UP AT ME WHILE I continue to slowly glide up and down his length.

I know I need to pick up the pace and ride him in earnest. We are on a time crunch, and I am being irresponsible. I smirk at him as I ignore his request. It won't be long until I have to take a six-week break from the delicious feel of him filling me, so I need to savor every glorious minute of it while I can.

"Close. So close," I respond.

We don't have long before the boys will wake from their nap. Ever since they turned two, they've taken to climbing out of the crib the moment they wake. Seems like Jake can't catch a break from the slippery twins. It secretly makes me happy when they get out and start to scatter. I love watching when he has to hunt them down as they hide from him in the house. But it also means they can just waltz on out whenever they wake, even during very inopportune times. We are currently two hours into their nap, and it's a ticking time bomb before we hear them storming down the hall.

Jake glides his hand up my thigh and nears where we are joined. He pauses and looks wickedly at me before he runs a finger through the wetness coating my sex. Using it, he slowly starts to rub circles on my clit, a move that he knows will bring me to climax within minutes.

"Move, darlin'," he says through gritted teeth, trying to hold his own orgasm off.

This might be one of the last times he's inside me for a while, and I just don't want it to end. Our baby girl is due this week, which means no sex during the recovery.

Knowing I'm purposefully being resistant to his demands, he instantly stops his torment on my clit. I rise up on him with the slowest of paces. I pause up on my knees with just the tip of his cock still inside me. Before I can continue my leisurely descent, Jake gives me a diabolical smile while snaking an arm around my body and smacking my ass. Shocked, I sink down on him hard, causing the orgasm I've been holding at bay to rip through my body just as Jake groans out his own release.

Spent, I slide off Jake and lie next to him on the bed, not bothering to clean us off me. It's not easy to be nine months pregnant and exert so much energy. I curl up against my husband, and my eyes start to close just as I hear the telltale sign that my two little men are up and ready for trouble.

"Nap, darlin'. I got them," Jake says as he pulls the covers over me. Then he ensures the door is closed before rounding the boys up.

After a two-hour nap, I wake refreshed and excited. In the en suite, my favorite part of our new house, I shower and put my favorite maternity dress on. It's blue with polka dots all over. It reminds me of the dress I wore to Bill's the night Jake took me.

I don't sing at Bill's anymore. Once I found Jake, my nights were all occupied. It was only a month after Jake confessed his love to me that we ended up at the courthouse. A week later, on our honeymoon, I found out I was pregnant. Six weeks after we returned, the doctor informed us that it was twins. Jake jokingly told me that he was cursed to chase Coletrain twins for the rest of his life. I quickly corrected him, reminding him I was a Blackwood now, and his kids would be, too. I swear he mumbled something about sneaky Coletrain blood under his breath.

The seedy bar was no place for me when pregnant, so I took a hiatus from the gigs while I prepared to be a mom of two. Never having had a mom of my own, I was unsure about everything I did. It wasn't until Hayden and Hunter turned one that Jake finally convinced me that being a mom was natural to me and I stopped second-guessing everything I did. I loved it, though I sometimes missed performing. I sing to my babies every night, but there is something about being on that stage, in front of a crowd, that makes my blood rush.

Shortly after the boys came, I made a funny lip sync video for Hannah's birthday and posted it on her Facebook wall. It was a compilation of all of my favorite Britney songs. She's always been my biggest supporter, and I wanted to thank her for everything in typical Millie style. It was Jake's idea to do the video instead of a live performance. He kept telling me how big the lip sync trend was and that a video was something Hannah would be able to watch over and over again. I was completely surprised when the video went viral on Facebook and Twitter.

With encouragement from Jake and Hannah, I started my own YouTube channel, and now, I post lip sync videos every Wednesday. I still do a lot of Britney, but I've diversified my interests to include a little *NSYNC, TLC, and even the occasionally Dixie Chicks song. The ad revenue my popular channel brings in means I can stay home with the kids. Jake still loves being a bail bondsman and makes a good living. He's the best and always gets his criminal. But he never went into it for the money. He loves the chase and the satisfaction he gets when he catches his guy. It is what he was born to do. I don't really miss my job. It was never my passion to work in a doctor's office. Now, I get to do what I love and be with the people I love every day.

I finish putting on my makeup and brushing my hair. Hannah, Tillie, and all of their brood are coming over for our weekly cookout. I walk out of our room and down the stairs, to where my three boys are waiting. I stand in the doorway and take in my family. Seeing Jake with his sons brings tears to my eyes. Silly pregnancy hormones. He is the perfect dad and the perfect husband. And, while I am not the perfect wife, my days of running are over.

Unless I'm running to Jake's bed, that is.

The End.

ACKNOWLEDGMENTS

Danielle Palumbo: You are priceless to us in so many ways. We can never thank you enough for all of your help— WITH EVERYTHING.

Our Betas—Nicole S, Nicole M, Danielle, Carli, Megan, Kelly: We still can't believe you guys read this and liked it. So thank you. And, if you lied to us, thank you for that, too.

To Our Husbands: Thanks for all the help with the research. ;)

To The Indie Author Community: We totally dig y'all's support.

Bloggers and Readers: You guys rock.

And, last but not least, to the young, skinny African American man in the Barnes & Noble in South Point Mall, we apologize for scarring you for life while in the process of plotting this book way too loudly.

ABOUT AMIE KNIGHT

Amie Knight has been a reader for as long as she could remember and a romance lover since she could get her hands on her momma's books. A dedicated wife and mother with a love of music and makeup, she won't ever be seen leaving the house without her eyebrows and eyelashes done just right. When she isn't reading and writing, you can catch her jamming out in the car with her two kids to '90s R&B, country, and showtunes. Amie draws inspiration from her childhood in Columbia, South Carolina, and can't imagine living anywhere other than the South.

WEBSITE: http://www.authoramieknight.com
NEWSLETTER: http://eepurl.com/cPHIuT
FACEBOOK GROUP:
https://www.facebook.com/groups/amieknightssocialites

facebook.com/authoramieknight

twitter.com/AuthorAmieKnigh

instagram.com/amie_knight

goodreads.com/AmieKnight

ABOUT MIRANDA ELAINE

Miranda is a loving wife and barely surviving mother of three occasionally good kids. Her hobbies include lying to herself about the calories in donuts and banana pudding, as well as running out of excuses when procrastinating. She's been an avid reader since she was a young girl. Whether she's by the pool, curled up in bed, or hiding in the closet, as long as she has a book in her hands she's happy.

WEBSITE: https://www.authormirandaelaine.com/
NEWSLETTER: http://eepurl.com/dou_3X
FACEBOOK GROUP:
https://www.facebook.com/
groups/mirandaelainesdonutsanddelicacies/

facebook.com/authormirandaelaine

twitter.com/authormirandae

instagram.com/authormirandaelaine

bookbub.com/profile/miranda-elaine

goodreads.com/Miranda_Elaine